I0520684

Jovian Heat

Karina L. Fabian

LASER COW
PRESS

Laser Cow Press
Merritt Island, FL

Laser Cow Press, LLC
Merritt Island, FL
www.fabianspace.com

Book Layout ©2017 BookDesignTemplates.com
Cover Art by Karina Fabian

Jovian Heat/ Karina Fabian.—1st ed.
Print ISBN #978-1-956489-04-0

Other Great Fiction by Karina Fabian

Science Fiction

Space Traipse: Hold My Beer, Season 1
Space Traipse: Hold My Beer, Season 2
Space Traipse: Hold My Beer, Season 3
Doall's Do-Over: A Space Traipse Story
The Old Man and the Void
Dex's Way
Discovery

Fantasy

Murder Most Picante: A DragonEye Story
If Wishes Were Dragons: A DragonEye Story
Mind Over Mind
Mind Over Psyche
Mind Over All

Anthologies with Space Traipse Stories

CRACKED: An Anthology of Eggsellent
Chicken Stories
Overmorrow: Stories of Our Bright Future
Planetary Anthologies: Neptune

To neonatal nurses

You are indeed heroes.

They say that if man were meant to live on Jupiter, God would have given him thicker skin and hydrogen-processing gills. That same "they" also said if man were meant to fly, God would have given him wings. Of course, by 2867, we'd not only cracked our genetic code, but could stack the nucleotides like gods playing with toy blocks. We gave ourselves wings or fins and gills and skins to suit any environment we wanted, and to hell with what God wanted. In the end, we could alter our bodies to suit, but we were still human, with the same noble desires to do what's right at war with the basest needs of our Fallen state. God wasn't letting us off so easy.

I sat at my desk with my feet propped up, staring out the window at the throng of life above and below me. The orange sky had taken on a reddish cast; the long-anticipated storm was coming at last, and while the meteorologists said it'd be a short one—only a couple of years—there were still whispers that Gravstead was going to be the next Red Spot. Looking at the number of movers on the flyways, I had to wonder if someone knew something I didn't. Not that I could afford to leave.

A sudden gust knocked a group of floating Jovians into traffic. Vehicles swerved. One bumped an unlucky floater, who fluttered off in the opposite direction, shaking his fist. I imagined a few obscenities in honor of our planet's namesake and his lovers were used.

I shook my head. Guppies.

When the geneticists designed humans for Jupiter's environment, they fell into two camps. One wanted to create super-dense molecular structures that could withstand the incredible atmospheric pressures—the heavies. The other decided a more elegant solution was an inflated barrier between dense skin and the more delicate internal organs—the guppies, because the amusing result was that they float instead of sink like us heavies would. But floating or walking, we were all just trying to get ahead in this gaseous soup we called home.

I pressed an oxygen mister against my gills and took another long drag. Yeah, I know. It'll kill me eventually, but I was celebrating. I'd just finished a case, digging up dirt on my client's soon-to-be-ex-husband, though with the tears on her arm fins, I would have thought she already had enough grounds for divorce. I dunno. Maybe her new boyfriend was beating her. She didn't seem like the type to have good judgement, and women did stupid things when they were in heat. It wasn't my business. She paid; I delivered. Now I was going to enjoy a good mist, then go hide away for a week.

The door chimed, and at my grunt, it irised open. Reed stepped in but hesitated at the threshold. He'd been my partner back when I was a beat cop. We used to patrol the lower levels. We'd saved each other's lives. After the last time he saved me—when I was in heat, in fact—I decided I needed more control over my own schedule. Now he's detective on the force, and I'm enabling women to make bad life choices. Not sure if I made the right life choice myself, but now and then, he came by to reassure me.

Looked like today was one of those times.

He'd always had a slouch, but it was even more pronounced than usual, and the grin of greeting he gave me was less than half-hearted. His eyes, normally sharp and so yellow they glowed, were tired, dull, defeated. I suppressed the urge to leave my desk and comfort him.

Whatever he was wrestling with, I didn't think it was going to be good for me. I wasn't about to tip my hand.

"You look like hell." I opened.

He didn't even snark back. I dropped my feet to the floor and leaned forward. "What is it?"

"I've got a case for you."

"Nope. Sorry. I'm off the clock. It's that time of the month."

When the geneticists designed Jovians, the women, guppies and heavies alike, ended up with one weird surprise. Once every six Earth-months, we go into heat. Yep, just like an animal, with all the overwhelming hormones and urges to go with it. They couldn't find a way around the problem—or maybe they just thought it was funny—so we Jovians were stuck with it. Eventually we adapted; in fact, without a better way of calculating time on our big, gassy world, we decided to use the female cycle to split the Jovian year into convenient months. Hence, 24 months in a Jovian year.

Convenient for telling time, but not much else. The human mind is more adaptable than an animal's, we don't turn into crazy mating machines. Still, it's easy to do something stupid when your brain is thinking how good the married man across the desk smelled at the moment. Or the perp who'd just as soon kill you as mate with you. Reed still had a scar from the last time my heat-addled brain made me freeze.

He'd always had my back, big hero. Just made the scar more sexy.

I squashed that thought fast before my gills started swelling. I wasn't stupid, anymore.

Reed hadn't even noticed my distraction, which said a lot for how tangled up he was feeling. He waved his pulse comp over the receptor on my desk. Obligingly, the desk projected a holo of a baby. I could barely tell what it was for all the tubes and special compression suits, but instinct said it was a girl. Her tiny little eyes swelled shut… I felt my gills constrict in sympathy.

"This is right up your alley, Cass. Simple paternity search, but it's gotta be done fast."

"Mix breed?" In the video, she waved her chubby fist. I fought the urge to coo.

"Gonna need a lot of expensive surgeries to survive. You need to find the daddy, make him live up to his obligation. I've been told to stay away from it."

I snorted. Reed was always a hero. You couldn't show him an adult in distress and expect him to walk away, much less a baby. I'd always admired that about him. Now, though, he had his own family to consider. The Captain must have threatened to fire him if he went snooping on his own time.

So I was his compromise between practicality and conscience. "What's going on, Reed? Where's the mom?"

He swiped left with a weary flick of his wrist. A dead Guppy draped flat over a jagged rebar, the heavy folds of her skin drooping like wet sheets, hiding her face. The tatts on her skin said she was a prostitute, licensed, mid-grade with seniority. The bar peeked from her back, brown and slick with blood. On the walkway below her feet, more blood congealed in a thick, mud-colored pool.

"No sign of foul play. This is that Pel factory they had to stop construction on because of the winds. It's along her route to her flat, a common shortcut for guppies. We figure she was passing through, and a gust blew her into the pole. Or… Well, we're not ruling out suicide, given her circumstances. We may never know for sure. She gave birth as she was dying."

I closed my eyes against the image. My heart and my uterus ached in sympathy. "I hate you, Reed. Fine. I'll do it. For the baby, but answer me one thing: We all have our genomes on file, so why isn't the hospital doing a genetics test and finding the father that way?"

"Oh, they did. Turns out the 'father' is Bobby Alberto Pel—except he's been dead for over a Jovian year."

* * *

Bobby Alberto Pel was the only son of Don and Mai Pel, whose family name graced half the machinery on Jupiter. Since their merger-by-marriage to the Hyatt clan, they were the second richest and most powerful family on the planet—and Jupiter is a big planet. I found article after article about the son's funeral. None ever mentioned the cause of death, just "complications of a long illness." He was survived by his parents and a sister, Ally.

I flipped through the public records but didn't find anything unusual. Bobby lived the charmed life of a genteel heavy: rode atmosteeds in the quads of his family mansion in Cleansedston, maintained a good but not stellar grade point average, participated in charitable activities—or at least stuck around long enough to have his holo taken at them. Most of the holos showed him with his best bud, Stone Hyatt. I didn't see any of him with his sister, though. Curious. Sibling rivalry, maybe? My own brother used to squish my gills until I learned to punch him in the gonads. Maybe such animosity didn't have economic limitations.

As interesting as my research was—and really, it wasn't especially interesting—nothing told me why anyone might want to inject Bobby's vaulted genetic material into a middling prostitute's womb.

The prostitute, registered as Kett, came up clean. Licensed, working for an independent establishment... Nothing unusual there. No diseases or history of violence or victimhood, a reasonable saving for someone in her line of work. She'd been fired with cause because of the pregnancy.

A gust of wind blew debris against the force field of my window, making it crackle. I glanced at the roads. What if Kett wanted out? Her savings wasn't enough, especially if she wanted to switch careers. Geneticists were still tweaking our genome—maybe one needed a carrier? Or maybe she thought a Pel baby was her ticket to the sweet life? Nah, not that. Where would a hooker get that kind of DNA in the first place?

I'd come to the end of what research would tell me. I needed to ask questions. I tapped my fingers on the desk. Parents or hookers first?

Hookers, while I was still early in my cycle. The last thing I needed was temptation. I dressed in a thick turtleneck with loose sleeves to hide the rosiness of my gills and forefins. The wind which may or may not have killed Kett was picking up, a blessing for me since it wafted away my leaking pheromones to mix with the regular stench of the city. As I made my way down the streets, I saw the guppies fighting to swim a straight course. I thanked Jove and the geneticists that I was born a heavy.

Kett had worked at the Leda, a tastefully garish club not too far from the business district. Kett had had a long swim to her flat, which suggested she had prioritized saving money. The façade was, of course, a replica of the famous Leda and Swan sculpture from Earth, and in the reds and oranges of the air, the building seemed to move suggestively, all the more so because of the winds. The door opened, releasing a heavy beat of music that rippled the air. Experience from years on patrol told me it was just within legal limits.

A heavy stepped out, sated and self-satisfied. I looked at her outfit and realized I had misjudged the clientele. I was underdressed. Didn't matter. I was there for work, and I'd probably be better off if I advertised the fact.

Inside was set up in the time-honored fashion of human brothels: Bar and dance club in the front, beauties of both genders gyrating suggestively behind colored force fields, a hall leading to private entertainment rooms in the back. Doxies, heavies and guppies alike, milled about, offering drinks and other services. The males took in my scent and gave me a mercifully wide berth. Females in heat usually came to such establishments seeking release with someone of their own gender. No risks of "accidents" that way. If I had wanted a male companion for the night (or hour), I'd have to sign a liability waiver.

I went to the bar, taking a seat where noise dampeners tamed the music and made conversation possible. I ordered a drink. I thought about getting an O2 boost, but I needed a clear head.

It didn't take long before one of the younger hookers took a stool beside me. Pretty thing, her smooth head marked with the tatts of her professional qualifications. More than I should have attracted. Guess she drew the short straw.

She set her hand on mine. "The heat stinks, doesn't it, honey? You wanna cool the burn, or just bitch about it awhile?"

I grinned, despite myself. I hadn't thought about someone paying for a girlfriend to complain to. Yet right now, it made perfect sense. Still, I shook my head. "I'm here about Kett."

The girl blanched. "Oh, Jove! I'm so sorry. Didn't you hear? She died yesterday."

"I know, but the baby survived—or may, if we can find her help. I'm looking for clues about the father. I'm Cassie Lane." I pointed my pulse comp at hers.

"Ruby," she replied, distracted by the information that showed up on her screen—just my basic PI information, license, the usual. Gotta be official. She looked up to the guppy bartender for guidance. She couldn't be older than two. This was probably her first job. I didn't blame her for being careful.

She flicked a nail at her wrist, sending my "card" to him. The bartender shrugged his fins, but he moved to a wall device and spoke into it. He was calling the boss. Good. I had a few questions for him, too.

"Is the baby okay?" she asked. I felt like she was genuinely concerned and not stalling for time.

"She's a halfbreed. She won't survive unless someone pays for some serious genetic restructuring."

"My cousin had a halfie. It was tragic. Did Kett know?"

"You tell me."

She shook her head. "Kett kept to herself. I mean, she is—was—really good at her job, and always willing to help one of us. I think we all cried on that big pillowy shoulder of hers. That was her thing, really. Listening. She made good money at it, too. She never talked about herself. Maybe she was afraid if she started talking, she'd let a client's secret slip. She had some very important clients."

"Any Pels?"

"Like the manufacturers, Pel? I really can't say. Client lists are confidential."

"Damn straight, they are." A guppy with gold-lined scales approached us, somehow inserting his presence between us without crossing the bar. He was not my type, but he oozed masculinity in that slimy way my former client would have probably found enticing. "You done fine, Ruby. I'll give you a bonus tonight. Go find a better client now."

"Thanks, Bo." She muttered a politeness about our chat, slid off the stool, and disappeared into the crowd.

Bo jumped right in. "Look, I'm really sorry about Kett and the baby. Kett was steady worker. But the Leda is a clean establishment. We abide by the statutes. We know the cycle of every female employee, and we schedule their clients appropriately."

I held up a hand to stop him. "I'm not here to toss lightning. I'm just looking for the daddy. Could she have been freelancing, or maybe had a boyfriend?" The last suggestion was more to give him a graceful out.

He didn't take it. "We pay our doxies well and we don't allow side jobs. Like I said, we work hard to ensure we offer clean services. And potential mates need to be registered and approved with the office."

"'Approved'?"

He met my sneer with one of his own. "It amazes me how some people still have such negative preconceptions about people in my line of work. Yes, approved. I run background checks and genetic screening on all my employees' relationship potentials. I care about my people."

"Aw, are they family?"

He rolled his eyes, and under the gold filigree, his scales took on a purple tinge. "Are you that cliché, or is it the hormones talking? They're not family. They're employees. Their job is to make the johns happy for a while. They can't do that if they've got bruises from some an abusive spouse or they're distracted by relationship problems."

"Can they have relationships, then?"

"Yes, of course. A couple are mated with kids. But Kett broke the rules. She got careless, she got gravid, and then instead of coming to me when we could have done something about it, she hid it for a month. You know how it is with guppies. You can barely tell until they're ready to pop. Then she had the nerve to tell me she didn't know how it happened. She broke contract, and she lied. She had to go. I wasn't happy about it, you know. She was a great employee, had a loyal customer base…and I liked her. I really did. I'm sorry about the stupid accident and about the kid being halfbreed."

The worst thing was, I believed him. I hoped that wasn't the hormones talking. "How did she feel about being let go? Was she despondent? Suicidal?"

"She was upset. Wouldn't you expect that? But I gave her a good severance package and letters of recommendation. She was never the stupid, helpless type. She had connections. She could have had the kid and gotten a new career."

"Could she have actually not known? Did she have any geneticists among her clients?"

"I can't give away client names."

"Thanks. Mind if I finish my drink? I won't question your employees."

He shrugged and left without a word. Probably a good thing. We almost shared a moment, there.

I nursed the drink and kept my back to the room—which didn't mean I wasn't casing the joint. Another cliché about bars: they always had mirrors. I guess it was a subtle hint to get your butt off the stool and go join the fun. The screens behind the shelves of drinks shifted between groups of happy people sharing jokes at tables, bodies twisting and rubbing together on the dance floor, couples or small groups leaning together as they made their way to the back rooms. I wasn't as badly dressed as I'd thought. There was quite a mix of classes, from the manufacturing district as well as the business sector. I saw a group that looked like they came out of Cleansedston. One brunette twisted her wrist to emphasize what she was saying, and her bracelets refracted the light in a way that said those gems were not just made off-planet, but actually mined out of alien ground.

The bulky form of the bartender cut off my view. "You didn't ask," he said.

I raised my brow along with my glass.

He filled it. "Ruby's a good girl," he said. "She wants to be like Kett, but I dunno. Kett had a gift. She could calm anyone down, make them feel right again. And she hardly spoke a word. I remember this one guy, some doctor. Stormed in, already half-drunk. Sobbing about his hands. He only had five fingers, but I didn't think that was the problem. Ruby tried to talk to him, and he shoved her. Bo and I were ready to float his heavy ass outta here, but Kett stopped us. She floated up beside him and waited. For an hour, he growled and sobbed, until he finally leaned on her shoulder. She had the best shoulders. She took him to the back. When they came out, he paid his tab and for her time, and apologized to Ruby. Never saw him again, and she never shared what he told her."

"Sounds like a good woman. So when was this? I mean, is Ruby that new?"

"Ruby is a lot older than she looks. She plays young and unsure. Some people like that. This was, wow, maybe a year ago? Anyway, just one of those stories about the kind of person Kett was, is all. Not that you were asking."

I settled my tab and left. Since I didn't know who was paying my bills on this one, I took the masstrans to the edge of Cleansedston. I'd have to get a private transport from there; the community would never stoop so low as to have walkways between homes, and I hadn't used a jetpack in nearly a year.

The masstrans was packed to the—pardon the pun—gills, and there was no room left in the isolation car reserved for ladies in their "time." I pulled my collar higher, gritted my teeth, and shoved myself into a corner, arms crossed and scowling to ward off any potential suitors who thought my public appearance was an invitation. Fortunately, the car was so crowded, no man thought it worth fighting the crowds as well as my demeanor. Still, I resolved to take a private car back home and send the bill to Reed. He owed me. I was supposed to be in my flat, enjoying a mist, a long soak and sappy holonovel.

At the last stop, I found a private flyer and hired it for the rest of the day. I told the robotic driver, "Pel mansion, and yes, I have business," and strapped myself in. The winds were picking up, buffeting my ride. The driver's news screen was showing a satellite image of Jupiter. The normal orange and red striations the planet wore with pride were swirling in our area. A deep red dot had started to form, with lighter bands of violent winds swirling around it. Gravstead was in the path of those bands. I really felt for the guppies who had to swim home. The path of the bands avoided one area where the original Red Dot had once been: Cleansedston. They were too rich and proper to deal with another storm.

I flipped open my private screen to search for five-fingered surgeons. Five fingers is not unusual, of course, but about a quarter of the population had eight—another fun genetic anomaly—and those that did gravitated to certain professions: programming, music, surgery.

When I didn't find any five-fingered surgeons working in Gravstead in the past two years, I expanded my search to genetic medicine...and wouldn't you know? Dr. Hoff Peters, genetic recoder...and the man whose name was on Bobby Pel's death certificate.

Then, the ride got too rough for reading. The automated driver called out a caution, and I obligingly turned off my screen and tightened my seatbelt. For the next 10 minutes, I sat in silence, my gaze alternating between watching the news screen and watching the thick soup of lighting-studded storm winds coursing around us outside. Even with noise-dampeners built into its hull, I could hear the howling wind and crashing thunder.

"How much farther?" I shouted so the driver could hear me. Unfortunately, it did not afford me the same courtesy.

"Reed, I hate you!" I grabbed the arm rests and fixed my mind on the image of a motherless baby with no one else to protect her from the ill winds of fate.

The barrier to Cleansedston practically crackled and flashed with activity as it fought to keep back the torrential weather that splashed against it, yet my car passed through without so much as a shudder. The sudden silence startled me even more than the boom of thunder had earlier. I realized then I hadn't been breathing properly, and I pulled down my collar to take in deep, calming draughts of air.

By the time I was calm enough to enjoy the view out my window, we were almost to the Pel mansion. By Jove, the place was amazing. Built on the second circle of Old Red Spot, where storms had cleared away the atmospheric debris, the place was paradise. I'd never seen air so clean. I almost had to squint against the brightness. In the stillness, you could see the subtle layering and interaction of chemicals. I'd learned in grade school that such things existed, but in the stirred-up soup of Gravstead, we never saw it. I'd only half-believed my teachers until this moment.

I could see for miles! It wasn't just the air. No tall buildings and heavy, blocky walkways marred my view. Everyone knew Cleansedston's motto: "Designed for living the way Jovians were designed to live." I understood it, now. Homes floated gently, without heavy restraints connecting them together and thick walls to protect against the eras-long zephyrs. Heavies lounged in floating chairs chatting to their guppy neighbors or zoomed by with jetpacks strapped to their backs.

In the distance, I saw another thing I'd only read about: an atmosteed. It was swimming a course, serene and beautiful, its long nose held proud, the fin on its back vibrating so fast, I could barely see it. Its white skin was lined with tan rings, and it held its tail curled under its belly. It looked just like the cover of my favorite childhood book.

The rider, a woman, leaned against its arched neck, urging it along. Her hair flowed, thick and brown. Mine never did grow back properly after shaving it for the police force, but even so, no one I knew had a gorgeous mane like that. The catty part of me wondered if it was Dr. Peter's work.

Another part of me wondered why it looked familiar.

Then we pulled up to the Pel's mansion, and I was forced to concentrate on the task at hand. How did you tell one of the most influential families on the planet that someone may have stolen their son's DNA to make a halfbreed baby?

Let's jump to the chase. I didn't do it well.

"How dare you?" Mai Pel exclaimed. She was a beautiful heavy, with ruddy orange skin and golden eyes, but at the moment, she was also one of the scariest females I'd ever seen. Beside her, her husband, Don, sat and stared at his hands. Had he always been so passive or had years of marriage cowed him into submission?

Mai didn't give me long to wonder. She continued, her voice haughty and powerful. "We would never be so careless with the Pel genome. My son died in this home. He was dissolved, in accordance with tradition, and released into the atmosphere. So unless you think you can get pregnant from the wind, you should turn your investigation elsewhere."

I wanted to duck my head, apologize and leave, that's how intimidating she was. I fixed my mind on the baby. "Dr. Hoff Peters signed the death certificate. Was he the attending physician? Was Bobby suffering from a genetic ailment?"

She didn't even answer. She just snapped her fingers, and robotic servants grabbed me under the armpits and tossed me out. Tossed. Through the open ceiling of their living room and onto the waiting platform of their porch. For a moment, I lay there on my back, staring at the stratosphere and wondering if I should be dismayed that one of Jupiter's genteel class could have such a violent temper or be impressed at the targeting abilities of her servants.

Then my view was obscured by a beautiful face with thick brown hair. "What did you say to my mother?"

"Ally Pel, I presume?" She backed away, and I sat up, then stood. Fortunately, that was not the first time I'd been tossed out of a place. I had landed on my back, which would ache, but that was better than a concussion.

Or maybe I was concussed. I turned to look at Ally and immediately felt hot and dizzy. By Jove and all his lovers, she was the most beautiful woman I'd ever seen. Her skin was ruddy orange like her mother's, but flawless, and her eyes shone like the description of the sun in some earth romance. While her mother projected Intimidating, Ally projected Rugged-and-Fun.

"You cannot be real," I exclaimed. Oh, yeah. I had to have hit my head.

Ally laughed and threw back her hair. I found myself mesmerized by the way it flowed. "Aren't you sweet? So, what did you ask my mother that got you thrown out?"

I shook my head to get it back into the game. I swiped my pulse comp to pass her my credentials. "I'm trying to find out about your brother's death. There's evidence suggesting his DNA may have been stolen, and I've been hired to follow up," I lied.

"Hired? By whom?"

Well, that was a suspicious question on two levels. "I can't reveal my clients' identities. But I'd think if it were the case, your parents would be interested to know if it were true. What do you know about the circumstances surrounding his death?"

Ally shook her head. "I hardly knew my brother. I was fostered to another family as a toddler. My mother was never especially good with children, as you can guess. I came home for his funeral. That's when I met Stone. We—it's a little embarrassing to admit —we hit it off right from the start, so our parents discussed it, and one month and some intense negotiations later, we married. I never learned much about my brother, even from Stone." She twisted her hands in the air in a kind of shrug. Something about it seemed familiar.

"What about your husband? Could he tell me more about Bobby?"

"I'm sure he could, but he's taking a tour of the storm's perimeter, trying to determine for himself just how bad it will affect Pel-Hyatt industries. He's very hands-on that way. In the meantime, I'm left here to amuse myself."

Then it clicked. "Is that what you were doing at the Leda? Amusing yourself?"

"I met some friends for lunchtime amusements. How did you know?"

"Not from the staff, if that's what you're asking. Are you a regular? Did you know Kett?"

Her friendly smile faded. "We all knew Kett. It's tragic about her death. She was easy to talk to."

"Did you 'talk' with her?"

"I think we all did some point. Is that a problem?"

"I guess that depends on your husband."

She sighed. "Not that it's any of your business, but Stone and I are friends, but there was never the romantic spark you see in holos. Our marriage was arranged, and we're content enough with it, but if, on occasion, we seek the comforts of someone more to our suiting…" She shrugged.

I held up a hand. "You're right. Not my business."

"But what about you, detective?"

"What about me?"

She stepped forward, and there was something very bold and decisive about the move. "Where do you find your comforts?"

She ran her forearm fin over my cheek.

For a moment, I was back in a dingy alley in the lower levels of Gravstead, a rookie beat cop in full heat, cornered by the very perp I'd been chasing. He'd run his fin over my cheek, and I was frozen. I knew I had to arrest him, had to fight, but all my body has wanted was to let him have his way, even if he decided to kill me afterwards.

I came back to reality with a terrified gasp. I stepped back fast, almost teetering on the edge of the porch. "Whoa! No!"

She, too, stepped away. "I'm sorry. I guess I misread."

"Yes, you did. Look, when you contact your husband again, can you please ask him to call me? It's imperative that I wrap this up fast."

"You sound like someone's life is at stake," she said.

Another suspicious comment. I didn't reply but whistled for my ride.

Once inside, I set the windows to privacy mode and pulled down my collar. I pressed my hands against my swelling gills. What was wrong with me?

I wanted nothing more than to soak in a metallic bath, burying myself in the liquid hydrogen and enjoying the pressure against my muscles. But I had the car until midnight, and I intended to get my money's worth, especially since I didn't know if someone else was paying. I told it to take me to Dr. Peters' office.

Peters had an office in the adjunct wing of the hospital, but the sign on his door said, "Closed for vacation" and a date 20 days from yesterday.

Yesterday, when Kett was found dead. I wandered over to the help desk and asked about him.

"Oh, he'd been planning that vacation for months," the receptionist told me. "He's such a nervous man, you know. I've been here six months, and I've never met anyone so precise. They say he made some mistake, probably as an intern—I mean, what intern doesn't screw up? It's learning. Still, since then, he's insisted on triple checking every calculation, every potentiality. He micromanages everything. He goes through staff like wipes, if you'll pardon my Mirandan. But there is no better genetic oncologist. Still, we're all so glad he's taking a little time to himself. He needs it."

She didn't know where he was going. He'd been very secretive about it. I thanked her for her time. Just as I was about to leave, maternal urges made me turn around.

"Um, where's the neonatal ICU?"

I told myself it was for the case. I needed all the information I could get. Maybe the baby had a clue, something no one else would see.

But really, I just needed to see her.

The holo hadn't done justice to her preciousness or the precariousness of her situation. She was swathed in nanotechnology that monitored the pressure of her organs, the hydrogen/helium mix of her blood, the erratic activity of her tiny beating heart as it struggled against the unforgiving god of a planet to push that blood through her system. She no longer had the strength to move her little fists, and her breathing came so fast and light, it was hard to imagine it was human breathing at all. I had no idea what the readings on the machines meant, but I knew what they were telling me. Find the father and make him pay!

"Marla's quite a fighter, isn't she?"

"What?" I jumped. The heavy nurse grinned at me. He was tall enough that I had to look up to see his golden eyes, but his shoulders were broad and the fins of his forearms wide and tinged a lovely purple. He had eight fingers on each hand. Four of the ones on the right were ensconced in a monitoring glove that I guessed connected to the baby's systems.

He jerked his chin toward the baby behind the field. "Marla. We all decided. If she was only going to be with us a short while, she deserved the honor of a name."

"That's…beautiful." I rubbed my burning eyes. I'd heard that oxygen breathers leaked water from their eyes. Tears, they called them. I wondered how it felt to do that naturally. The only time Jovians shed tears was when they overdosed on mist.

"Are you okay? You're not a reporter, are you? It's just, we were told not to discuss her case. I can get you the name of our press liaison…"

"No, no, I'm not. I—have reporters come by?"

He shook his head. "Not on my shift. It's like they were warned away. So, who are you, then? Not some ICU groupie?"

Why weren't there reporters? "Groupie?"

He blushed. He was cute when he blushed. "Sorry. Bad joke. You know, us ICU nurses are such heroes… So…?"

"Oh, sorry. I'm Cass. Cassiopeia Lane. Um, here." I swiped him my card.

"I'm Gree Peshion. Oh, you're a PI! Now, that's heroic."

"Not the way I do it. But I'm trying to figure out who or where the father is."

"They didn't tell you? It's supposedly some guy dead fourteen months."

"They told me. But just 'cause he's dead doesn't mean he's not the father."

Gree's eyes widened. "Artificial insemination? But why? I mean, the father was a heavy. Why not find a heavy for the mother?"

I took a step toward the isolation shield that separated us from Marla. "I don't know. Nothing about this makes sense..."

One of Marla's alarms beeped, and I jumped. "What's that? What's wrong?"

The fingers of his right hand danced over virtual controls he knew kinesthetically. "Easy. Just a minor adjustment. She's not leaving us yet."

"She shouldn't leave us at all! I'm going to find the sonnovaplute that did this to her, and I am going to make him pay."

I gripped my fists tight and squeezed my eyes shut against the whirlwind of emotions. Jove and all his lovers, I hated the weird mix of need and despondency warring in me.

Then, Gree's hands were on my shoulders, and I could feel my blood pulsing under his gentle grip. I could smell his sweet, strong scent, my gills flared to take it in. I opened my eyes to meet his beautiful yellow ones, and the air between us held more electricity than the storm outside.

I shivered.

Then he broke away. "Oh, Jove. I'm sorry. I'm so stupidly oblivious."

"No," I stammered. "No, it's okay. I get it, I—"

"I didn't mean to take advantage. You were sad, and I —"

"No, you didn't. It's my fault. This stupid case... I mean, it's not stupid. I just..."

"Bad timing?"

"The worst." I let out a giggle that sounded a little hysterical even to my hormone-ringing ears. "You know? I should go. I need to follow up on a lead. There's so little time. I just wanted to..."

"Find some motivation?"

Raging heat aside, I wanted to kiss him for that insight.

Maybe he noticed. He glanced away, shyly. "Okay, so I have your contact information. How about if I let you know if there are any changes?"

"Could you?"

He nodded, and I decided to end on that note before I acted on my stupid first and second impulses. Five steps down the hall, I had a third impulse I decided wasn't so stupid. "Gree?"

He'd already turned his attention back to Marla and her monitors, but he paused to raise a brow.

"No matter what happens, call me in a week, anyway?"

I headed to my car feeling much better. Giddy, even. PIs are heroes, Gree had said, or something close to that, and I wanted to be a hero for that little girl—and her attractive neonatal nurse.

I had the car take me home. Much as I wanted a pressure bath, I settled for a quick, cool sonic shower and a change of clothes. Something in mottled colors to blend in with the twilight. Then I downed some coffee for the stimulant. Jovians had been engineered to prefer the nine-and-a-half-hour days of our world, but there was enough human in us to stay up three, four, even five days if needed. Right now, Marla needed my every waking moment. I grabbed my equipment and my gun and headed out.

As befitting one of the top genetic surgeons in the hemisphere, Peters' house was near the hospital, but in its own cube of territory, floating free like a Cleansedston home, but fully enclosed against the weather. What I didn't expect was to see light and movement in one window. Was he actually taking a staycation and not skipping town?

I rang the chime once, and then again. There was no answer. I pressed a listener against the door. It was one of my less official but most useful devices. It read the changes in air pressure on the other side of a barrier and translated them into sound or visuals. In this case, it showed me the heavy as he spun, his five-fingered arms in the air. He had something in his hand. He pressed it against his gills, then crumpled. I heard the thump.

Twenty days, staying home? Panic rose in me, and I used my lock pick to hack the alarm and let myself in.

Hoff Peters lay in a puddle on the ground, and I mean puddle. Water was leaking from every orifice. Actual H_2O.

"No!" I told my pulse comp to contact emergency services and rushed to him. I yanked the mister from his hand and forced him to roll onto his side. I lifted his hips up, so that his butt was higher than his gills. It's super awkward, and usually took two people, but I managed by using furniture to prop him up. This was not my first time I'd seen someone OD on oxygen.

As I hoped, he vomited water and even more came spilling out his left gill. He gasped. "Please, go. It's too late."

"Like hell. You're going to live, confess to the police, and then make right by that baby. Why would you make a mixed breed just to let her die?"

"Baby? No, that...not me. Bobby... Bobby..." He paused to vomit but gurgled instead. The oxygen he'd forced into his system was reacting too fast to the hydrogen in his lungs and blood. Where was that ambulance?

"What about Bobby?" I demanded.

He forced himself into a sitting position. "Bobby is alive...but not Bobby. Stone doesn't know, I think. My fault. My fault. I suppose the baby, too."

"What do you mean, Bobby isn't Bobby?" I stopped to wipe at an itch on my nose.

"Leave. Run. Not OD."

"What does that mean? Tell me about Bobby." I shook him, but it was too late. I was left with unanswered questions and a corpse with a frozen grin and tears in his eyes.

"Hera's rivals!" I swore and shoved him for good measure. Nonetheless, I felt tranquil. Weirdly so. I wiped at a tickle on my nose, and it came away wet. Water, wet.

Not OD.

Oh, Jove!

I tried to stand, but I was lightheaded. What a funny phrase, considering my body was filling with water. Peters must have been a casual O2 user, sure, but that hadn't killed him. Someone had flooded his house with oxygen, and I'd been breathing it in, too.

I forced myself to standing, using furniture to brace myself. Oxygen was heavier than Jupiter's natural hydrogen; I'd find better air standing. I staggered and lurched from couch to chair to table. I coughed and spit and cried, and no, it was not a pleasant release like in the novels.

The hallway was narrow. I could lean on it and stagger to the door. If I could just cross from the table to the wall.

I lurched, stumbled, missed. Now that I understood the situation, I could almost feel myself drowning in the air. My gills tried to expand, but I clamped my hands over them and crawled on my knees toward the hall. I had the crazy thought that I should thank my brother; all his bullying had taught me to hold my breath and think past pain and fear.

Then the door burst open, and emergency medics rushed in.

"Oxygen," I croaked, "in the air."

I was vaguely aware of a woman, a guppie, swooping me into her arms and floating me out. I found it funny that she didn't seem the least bit attractive. There was a clue there, I thought. Then I thought no more.

* * *

I woke up in a detox chamber. My body floated in a large tube filled with liquid metallic hydrogen designed to compress the water out of my system. Only my neck and head were exposed to air, and small fans lined the collar of my cushion to draw away the moisture.

I laughed. I finally got my bath.

"Glad you find it funny." Reed moved into my field of vision to glare at me. He looked reassuringly handsome. "Jove and his mistresses, Cass. When I gave you this case, I didn't mean for you to get killed over it."

"Oh, good, because I haven't."

He rolled his eyes. "What were you doing at Peters' home?"

I couldn't turn my head. "Anyone else here? No? Good. Peters was murdered —that much is obvious, right? I think it has to do with Kett. Did anyone check Kett for DNA that wasn't hers?"

"Like a struggle? You think Peters killed her? Why?"

"No, I think she was killed, by the same person who killed Peters. People. Maybe the scary mom?"

"What? You're delirious still."

"No, sorry. Just thinking. Look. I'm close to solving this case. I just need evidence. I don't want to ask you…"

He waved my protest aside. "Don't worry about that. The storm is going Red Spot. This city will be a ghost town in a month. We're leaving as soon as we can save up enough for transport. If I lose my job over this, I can pack between odd jobs."

Red Spot? What about Marla? I pushed the thought aside. Save her life, then figure out her future. "Okay. I need you to find the records on the Pels. Mai, Bobby, Ally. Especially Ally. Where she was fostered, where she went to school. That stuff."

"Why?"

"Ally's too damn attractive."

He looked at me like I was nuts or dying or both. "I'm calling the nurse."

"Actually," a familiar voice said. "I'm right here."

"Hey!" Even under the cool, controlled pressure of the bath, I felt myself warm to Gree's presence. "Why aren't you with Marla?"

"Came to see my second-favorite patient."

Reed looked from my stupidly grinning face to Gree's equally besotted one. "Ooookay. I'm going to go look up those things for you, and you get coherent so you can explain all this."

I hardly noticed his exit. "So, how is she?"

Gree's smile waned. "She needs genetic recoding in the next four days, or we won't be able to reverse the damage. We're doing everything we can. What can I do for you?"

He was so sweet. I wanted to stare into those eyes forever. "Could you look up some medical records for me? I saw a birth certificate for Ally Pel. Can you tell me how long her mom, Mai, was in the hospital, and if there were any complications with the birth? And… What do you know about transgender recoding?"

"You're not thinking about…? Is it really that bad?"

"What? No. It's PI stuff. I wouldn't. I'd never…" Then my brain caught up. He was teasing. "Oh, you!"

His grin made my heart skip. When he left, he set my pulse comp to voice commands. I called up video on Bobby and Stone. There was quite a lot of it—charity events, society parties, sports competitions. The two were inseparable, always roughly nudging each other. Bobby had a tendency to talk with his hands and often smacked his friend by accident, particularly when he did that funny twist of his wrist.

The wrist? No… Could it be? I called up footage of Ally and Stone at their wedding. He always kept control of her hand closest to him, holding it, nestling it behind his back. But there was the nudging, gentler, and… Yes, there was the twist.

I laughed with relief so hard I leaked tears. It did feel good.

Laughter turned out to be the best medicine for detox. That, and the motivation of a sick baby and a case about to crack. The information Gree and Reed found was all I needed. I got out of detox in record time and swore never to mist again, as well. As soon as I got out of the bath and had dressed, I called Reed and asked him to escort me to the Pel estates.

Stone had apparently returned, and the family was all out for a ride. We waited on the wide veranda while a servant fetched them.

"I could get used to living like this," Reed muttered.

"If that storm is everything it says it's going to be, we won't, but maybe your great-grandkids will," I replied.

"Just our luck, eh? Hey, will you look at those?"

The Pels and Stone brought their atmosteeds straight to us. Mai sneered down at me. "I already had you evicted. Why are you harassing us again?"

"We're here for Bobby," I replied.

"That's not funny!" Stone exclaimed. The Pels, however, were furiously yet suspiciously silent.

"So Peters was right," I said. "You don't know."

"Shut up," Ally said, even as Mai snapped her fingers.

Reed however, held up a police override device. Her mechanical foot soldiers stopped a respectable distance away.

"Whatever you have to say, you can say it in the presence of our lawyer," Mai countered.

I grinned. "I'm not police. By Jovian law, I can make accusations in the presence of the authorities and let all of you sort it out. Or, Ally, you can come clean to your best friend and husband."

Ally glared at me with narrowed eyes—and by Zeus' bolt, xe looked good.

Don said, quietly, "Stop now. Whatever price you want, we will pay, but silence your tongue."

I actually hesitated. Any price? I could demand they help Marla. He could do it, no questions. They could make it some kind of charity thing. The Pel-Hyatts would look like heroes, and Marla would live. I'd take her—or Reed could. He and his wife always wanted more kids.

Why stop there? The storm was getting worse. They were evacuating Gravstead, for at least three generations. "Any price" could get Reed a sweet place in calmer climes for him and his family. And me—I could leave and take Gree, if he'd come.

Reed wasn't even supposed to be here. He'd hired me so he could see justice while keeping his name out of it.

But that was the crux, wasn't it? Justice. There was a dead woman and a dead doctor. What was their price?

I answered my own question. "Let's start with Bobby. Stone's best friend and the only child of Don and Mai Pel. Bobby's birth wasn't easy, was it Mai? Afterwards, you weren't able to have any more children."

"Ridiculous!" Stone protested. "Ally—"

"Ally, who was never seen before the wedding. Ally, who has no records outside some sparse official transcripts and a birth certificate - signed by Doctor Hoff Peters, a genetic surgeon, not an OB. Born in a hospital, yet there are no records of Mai having been in the hospital at that time. Ally, who did not exist until Bobby was no more."

"How did Bobby die?" Reed asked.

"He...was sick," Don said. Wow, he was an awful liar. Mai must handle all the business negotiations.

"Of course, he was sick," Stone said, his conviction stronger for his ignorance. "I couldn't see him for months before he died. We spoke over chats and holos…"

I said, "So sick his best friend could not see him, yet he never went to the hospital, or to his family physician. Instead, you brought in Peters, whose specialty is recoding DNA. What kind of disease requires your genes to be rewritten?"

"Dr. Peters is one of the leading experts in cancers and noble gas deficiencies," Don started.

"Yeah, now. Eleven months ago, his field was transgender mutation."

Stone twisted to look at his wife. His face contorted with a mix of confusion and horror, but not quite surprise. "Oh, Jove-as-a-bull. Bobby?"

Ally, nee Bobby, rolled xer eyes. "You are all so dramatic. Yes, fine. I had transgender recoding. You knew I was always curious. How many times did we joke about my femaling up? This should not be a such a shock. Really, I'm surprised you didn't figure it out yourself. We've been married a year."

"Fourteen months," I interrupted. "And that's the key, isn't it? By Jovian marriage contracts, for the first year of marriage, divorces are no-fault. If

Stone had found out before then, you could have simply separated and no harm done to the family fortunes. But once that anniversary passed, your little lie could cost your family everything."

Ally leaned toward xer husband and brushed xer hair over xer shoulders. "But you wouldn't have done that, would you, honey? I mean, our marriage was always one of friendship and business."

"Maybe," Stone replied. He pressed a hand against his gills and refused to look at his wife. "Maybe if you'd told me."

Ally bit xer lip and snuck a glance toward xer mother. It was the same kind of look Ruby had given the bartender, was it only two days ago?

"Momma didn't let you, did she? Too worried about the family fortune. Pel Industries is huge in Gravstead and for thousands of kilometers westward...all in territories soon to be demolished by the Red Spot Storm. The territory would be another Cleansedston in a century, so you'd be rich, but you had to weather the storm. Your family needed an alliance, and Stone Hyatt was the perfect match, with Hyatt interests across the inhabited planet and strong business savvy. So you 'femaled up' in secret, faked your death, and came back as Bobby's estranged sister. A convenient lie for a convenient marriage.

"But much as you enjoyed playing girl, something wasn't quite right, was it, Bobby? I had a long talk with a…friend…about genetic recoding. Sometimes, it doesn't take. A part of you is still male. That's why you prefer the company of females, even in your female form. Remember what you said to me: 'more suitable companionship?' That part of you that is still male, unlikely and miniscule as it may be, nonetheless reacted to Kett's heat and did what any thick-blooded Jovian male would do. You hired her for sex. She thought she was safe, of course, but somewhere in that mingling, your body found a way to impregnate her."

"Don't be disgusting!" Mai boomed.

"There's nothing disgusting about two bodies following their genetic imperative. The disgusting part, you three orchestrated." I clenched my fists to regain my temper.

"We have the genetic evidence, and a simple paternity test will prove or disprove my hypothesis, which should be easy, since you've admitted to being Bobby. The question is, which of you murdered Kett?"

"What?" There was a three-way gasp of outrage from the genteels. Only Don remained silent, and he looked positively sallow. I felt really bad for him. Still, I continued. "Kett figured it out, too, didn't she? Maybe you let something slip during pillow talk. Maybe she remembered the night Peters came in, despondent, crying that he'd failed. The mistake he made, the one that drove him to change career focus and grow hyperattentive to details—people thought it was a failed surgery, but it was you. He knew the recoding hadn't completed.

"Or maybe Kett just thought you would help her, but when she contacted to you, pregnant and asking for money, you jumped to conclusions. You agreed to meet her at the destroyed construction zone. You pushed her into the rebar and left her deflated and helpless."

"We found DNA at the crime scene." Reed was bluffing. You don't do DNA collection of an accident or suicide. By the time I'd suggested murder, the winds had swept any evidence away. Still, you'd never know from the steady way he met their eyes.

Ally/Bobby cracked first. "I told you we should have paid her off."

Xer father sighed. "Son, shut up."

"What?" Mai's eyes widened in shock and horror, and I felt my own stomach sink in surprise. She hadn't done it? It was Don and Bobby?

"No," Stone moaned. He swayed in his saddle but kept his seat.

"Stone, I'm sorry," Ally/Bobby said. "I was doing it for the family. For us. They would have destroyed everything worse than the storm."

"They?" Reed asked.

"Son, shut up!"

Don dismounted onto the veranda platform. "We're not saying anything more until our lawyer is present. If we come peacefully, can there be a minimum of fuss, please? I would prefer not to alarm the neighbors."

Reed whistled, and the car obligingly pulled up next to the platform. Don and his child went in quietly. Mai dismounted as well, but she strode straight to me. She slapped my face hard enough to leave a welt.

"If you think your little theatrics are going to guilt this family into helping that halfbreed pup,

think again. You have destroyed my family—
every generation!"

Then she stormed away, presumably to call
the family lawyer.

Through it all, Stone sat, unmoving, on his
atmosteed.

* * *

I accompanied Reed to the station and stayed
long enough to give my statement, and then to
stand at attention with him while the captain
alternately chewed us out for sticking our noses
where they didn't belong and congratulating us
on solving a double homicide. Part of me wanted
to snicker, it was so much like the old days. Part
of me wanted to correct the captain that it could
end up a triple homicide.

I wanted to throw myself into Gree's arms and
sob until my heart broke and the storm took me
and Marla and the Pels and the whole damn
world. But Gree was working, and I wasn't going
to embarrass myself. Instead, I staggered
through gale-force winds to my office, and dug
into the drawer for my mister. I stared at it, my
hands shaking. I looked at the pretty little device,
but I just saw Peters' macabre smile and every
orifice of his body leaking.

I threw the mister against the wall and sunk to the floor, sobbing.

When I could finally think again, I washed my face, straightened my collar, and made the difficult, gusty trek to the hospital. I had to tell Gree, I'd solved the case and failed the baby. I had to tell Marla I was sorry.

I found the ICU bustling with activity. Orderlies brought in equipment, directed by nurses. Gree and one of his coworkers leaned over Marla, doing I-didn't-know-what. In one corner, a doctor talked to Stone Hyatt.

The doctor caught me staring and started to order someone to escort me out, but Stone stopped him. He came over to me. "Miss Lane."

"Cassie," I said.

He nodded but didn't correct himself. "I...am not happy with what has happened, or with your unorthodox methods. Nevertheless, I am a man of honor. I married Ally Pel, and I vowed to share our responsibilities as well as the benefits of our union. This child may not be mine, but if it is indeed Ally—Bobby's—then it is family."

"She. Marla is a girl—an actual female."

We walked to the force field together. They were moving Marla to a different kind of isolation chamber. I guessed it was one designed for genetic recoding.

Stone said, "Yes, the doctor had said the staff named her. It's a good name. Ally and I couldn't have children. Now I know why. I always wanted a daughter. She'll have to be a fighter if she's going to be a Pel-Hyatt."

"She is."

Gree looked up, saw us, and smiled. Then he reached into the isolation chamber and scooped the tiny babe into his arms. At that moment, she had no wires attached to her body, no tubes stuck into her nose or veins. When he tilted her so we could see her face, she opened her mouth in a weak yawn.

I turned into complete mush, and I vowed to marry Gree and have all his heavy babies. I didn't think that was stupid at all.

It doesn't matter how we mess with the genome, there's no escaping human nature. We still love and hate, fight to defend our families, and kill to protect our reputations. We redesigned ourselves to live in the most hellish environments, and we still managed to find a slice of heaven in them. And when our noblest natures shine through our basest states, God smiles.

- Please review this on Goodreads or Amazon. You don't have to say much. Any feedback is appreciated.
- Sign up for my newsletter to learn about new books: https://tinyurl.com/fabianspacenews.

Thanks for Reading!

This was not a story I'd intended to write. Several of my writing friends had been talking about this cool anthology series, with one book for each planet in the system, plus Mars and the Moon. It sounded like a great challenge, and I do love anthologies.

Several of us in the Catholic Writers Guild SFF group took up the task, writing and sharing our stories in critique. My thanks to those friends who made this story worthy of the anthology.

The anthologies are going out of print this year (2022) but I loved the stories so much I'm giving them new life as stand-alones. Thank you for taking an interest in my work. I hope you enjoyed Cass's adventure as much as I did.

About the Author

Karina Fabian lives on Ground Zero for potential Xindi attack, but she can watch rocket launches from her front yard, so that's a plus. In 1990, she married a steely-eyed spaceman, Rob, who is now the COO of Vaya Space. She writes fictional space travel while he works to make it true. In the meantime, they raised four great kids.

Karina also writes fantasy and comedic horror and creates themed journals (the kind you fill in) for fun. Check out her offerings at https://karinafabian.com.